T0121015

THE BOOK OF CHRISTIAN

NICHOLAS GRIFFIN LOMBARDI

authorHOUSE®

AuthorHouse™
1663 Liberty Drive
Bloomington, IN 47403
www.authorhouse.com
Phone: 833-262-8899

Published by AuthorHouse 12/13/2022

ISBN: 978-1-6655-7805-9 (sc)
ISBN: 978-1-6655-7804-2 (e)

Print information available on the last page.

This book is printed on acid-free paper.

(1) (1) I'm going to tell you about the Christ,

(2) One day there was born to Adam and Tricia Spalding a boy named Christian. He was an accident, they didn't plan on Him, and He was born 14 months after His older brother Thomas. (3) Christian was a special boy from the beginning— strong, curious, mercurial. (4) It was as if He didn't quite belong even from the beginning although He was His mother's favorite. (5) He was beautiful, the most beautiful among His two brothers. He was a 10, Thomas a 6, Eric His younger an 8. (6) Christian was conceived in Boston, delivered in Philadelphia, spending time in Boothwyn, Pennsylvania, Delaware, Lancaster and Fort Washington, Pennsylvania in childhood. (7) Thomas and Christian were best friends, puzzle pieces; Thomas pragmatic, outgoing to a fault, Christian thoughtful, pensive, calculated. (8) One time Christian made Thomas cry, He would never forget it; during an angry moment He threw a ketchup bottle through the air striking Thomas

on the leg near the knee. (9) He was a bit of a cry baby, dramatic; Christian wasn't a cry baby, He was tough and something in Him knew it. Something in Him always felt the stronger one. (10) He remembers His father always seeming to lean on Him over Thomas when it came to menial work as if he knew Christian just had it in Him. (11) He liked this. (12) At the doctors the other boys would scream and make a fuss over shots, Christian would, the strangest thing, would just look at the arm silent, waiting and looking on as the needle was inserted, saying nothing. (13) When the kids were spanked it was the same; Thomas would yell and cry, Eric would scream in terror, Christian in the oddest way— silent. Not just for one spanking, every single one— silent. (14) Pulling up His pants as it finished and walking to His room. He liked Thomas though, he never made Him feel like a younger brother and in a certain way He was admired by Thomas, looked up to in a sense; a father, older brother in a sense. (15) They shared friends and like I said they just fit they really just fit— grand chemistry.

(2) (1) Christian was religious. (2) One day it was 7th grade, the end of the school year, He had never kissed a girl, He thought to meet up with one of His girl friends in the hallway to kiss before the year let out. (3) He remembers kneeling down literally on the steps of His second floor middle school on His way back upstairs, "God if You would just give me this have her walk out of class." (4) He got up, climbed the rest of the staircase, walked past the classroom door, door opens up, Michelle, as He prayed exactly. Shocked, He found strength only to say hello.

(5) He went to a devotional lesson when He was 14 given by His church youth group pastor. (6) "Jesus is saying here you either give 100% or you don't at all," the preacher went on on Revelation chapter 3. (7) Christian sat and thought God reasonable as He heard God's admonishment to shit or get off the pot as it were. (8) He sat registering Himself out of the categories "lukewarm" and said to Himself, "If I'm gonna do this and follow God, I'll do it with everything, be a soldier, as it should be,

but right now I don't want to; I haven't seen the world, if He'd rather me against Him than half way for Him, I'm out." (9) That night as He rode home He thought to Himself about this shift and began things right away. (10) It was in school that things got practical. (11) He made new friends, this time with the potheads. (12) In time He was smoking weed, sneaking around with girls and being a badass. (13) He did this for 6 months until Pittsburgh. (14) His youth group pastor invited Him there for the weekend. (15) He agreed to go, wanting some time away from home. Soon, He found Himself with Todd Wright and Sam Clement, college students— the closest things to Christians He'd ever met. (16) They were genuine, cool, funny, everything church wasn't normally; Christian's wheels turned as He saw their lives. (17) More importantly Christian saw God's hand in things as He sat with these "hot," fully committed Christians, "If I do this I'm really going to do this," He remembered saying. (18) He was in love; He identified with their lives and choices, saw and gloried in God's hand and decided

He would do it. (19) He would change His life around 180; leaving the potheads to become this real Christian He knew existed in His heart. (20) After one last girl to make-out with summer of 8th grade, He gave it all and began this relationship with God full force, changing everything.

(21) He was popular in 8th grade being a badass, but now He had no one, maybe if you spoke to Him you would understand, but an onlooker would have thought He was visited by aliens or something strange. (22) He pulled away from the potheads and survived. (23) High school was a blur, He cared little for it, couldn't wait to be out. (24) Soon He was out and on to the next thing. He was off to college, Nashville, Tennessee.

(3) (1) College was a time of growth, He was the president of a campus ministry and grew out of His shell, out of His quiet, insecure, tendencies. (2) By the end of college He was strong, ready for the world. (3) He moved to Boston, Massachusetts, and one day prayed to God, "God I want You to unify all Christians

into one movement, and I want to lead it." (4) The next day He was reading His Bible and felt the hand of God speaking to Him: "If You do what I command You like David did, I will be with You like I was with David, I'll build You a house like I built him and will give Israel to You." (5) So He was chosen by God to lead a movement. (6) Soon He left His church and everything He knew to follow the calling. (7) He had left His church because He couldn't swear around them. (8) He had learned not that swearing should be done for swearing's sake, but that it wasn't words themselves that were foul in speaking, but it was how and why you said what you said that made speech good or bad; and that any rule against this, that got in the way of this, caused trouble and got in the way of people and relationships. (9) He found power in this new revelation and though He was an outcast and seemingly uncool in high school that He was now cool and cooler than those not following God. (10) It was because Christian said "fuck" and meant it, He didn't do it for some bullshit reason. (11) On Facebook

He began to use these words; soon He found Himself at odds with His church friends. (12) Since He was a no-bullshit Christian since 8th grade He became popular in His church, the most popular of any His age but after using "fuck" and "shit" and spreading His wings for God in this way He lost popularity. (13) A Prince once among this people, He was now alone like anyone else, like Joseph sold out by his brothers. (14) But Christian kept going He knew God was with Him, He had to keep going, He knew it would work out.

(4) (1) Soon He met a girl. (2) One day He was invited (before leaving His church) to go over a friend's house from the church. (3) He remembers walking in and though it was the person who took Him to the friend's house that had a romantic interest, He was struck by the girl in front of Him at this house—Claudette Green. (4) He saw her face and the first thing He said in His heart was, "Who is this pretty girl?" (5) Claudette was taken aback by Christian's demeanor; His powerful mix of strength, sincerity and genuineness and was

left with an impression she wouldn't forget. (6) Christian remembers His friend jealous as she caught wind of this new apparent flame.

(7) Claudette was His friend and one day weeks after their first encounter wrote Him. (8) "Christian, I know people have been treating You a certain way, just know if You need someone to talk to I'm always here. It was great meeting You weeks ago, I was taken aback by Your energy and aura, let me know if You want to meet, xxx-xxx-xxxx." (9) Christian looked at the message warily, "Is this girl for real or just trying to get in My pants?" He decided to get back to her; she was pretty, yes, but He was in no way looking to move anything forward. (10) There came a day that He texted her though, He was in Boston and decided to text her to meet up. (11) She acquiesced and met Him for coffee. (12) "So with this new cursing thing, You think You would like swear from the pulpit?" She asked wide-eyed. (13) The two talked and Christian felt a certain sincerity from her. (14) Before eating their food Christian took both her hands and said a prayer. She was gone;

with His strength, His willingness to stand for something, His confidence to take her hands without asking, His willingness to take the lead, she knew she found someone she could love and trust. (15) Before they said goodbye, Christian told her of His love back home, Sarah Kingsford. (16) Him and Sarah had fallen in love in Nashville in college. She was a black girl, busty and curvy. (17) It had taken Christian about a year and a half to admit to Himself that He liked her but in time in college He did and they were in a sense a dating couple. (18) Sarah had decided to break things off with Christian before He left for Boston, but Christian knowing that God had told Him they would be together stayed faithful to her in His heart. (19) Fully committed to Sarah, it was easy for Him to keep things in a friendly place with Claudette, to Claudette's disappointment.

(5) (1) Christian now had left His church completely. (2) With this new swearing revelation He felt personally strong like never before and He knew His church would not accept it. (3) So now on His own in Boston

He said goodbye, choosing God and what was right over His old friends. (4) He was also anointed with oil on the same day He was called. He had by "chance" bought olive oil at the store and decided to rub it all over as a health remedy for skin. (5) After applying it over everything inch of Him, He got down on His knees knowing that God had just anointed Him, "Did You just anoint Me with oil?" He said to God and in love and admiration got down on His knees, worshipping.

(6) He had told Claudette during their second meeting over coffee about what happened with the calling. (7) "Yeah He called Me, I was reading my Bible, all of a sudden I'm reading a verse from 1 Kings, God was speaking to a new king, King Jeroboam, He said, 'If you follow My commands like David did I will be with you like I was with David,' I was reading and mind you I had just prayed, "God if You would let Me, let Me lead this movement." (8) "I was reading Claudette, all of a sudden My eyes go right to that verse, not above it, not below it, right on it and I just knew I was

being spoken to by God Himself answering My prayer." (9) Hearing about His willingness to leave His church, essentially His whole life behind Him for what was right Claudette was inspired, feeling uninspired by her church and she also decided to leave. (10) Having heard of this new movement Christian was called to start, 2 weeks after the coffee where she heard this, she texted Him, "Hey I left the church, if You've started any meetings or anything let me know." (11) Christian, knowing it was for God that He had left everything, was thrilled as He started to see God perhaps giving Him a first member. (12) A church where all Christians could be one like He had prayed.

(6) (1) Christian met with her again at a bagel shop. (2) He remembers her face, "It was as if pink hearts were shooting out of her from the back of her head," as she sat with Him wide-eyed as He talked to her about life and what God was doing. (3) Christian found strength though in His position with Sarah and didn't respond but kept Claudette in check. (4) His strength and though being attractive, not

treating her in a romantic way, in a sense His way of keeping things "about business" with Claudette only made her like Him more. (5) On the train He remembers Claudette after being still more attracted to Christian, laying her head on His shoulder. (6) Christian, aroused by this and made uncomfortable, at first said nothing. (7) In the car when she drove Him home she was playful, perhaps flirting with Him, "Stop flirting with me," Christian said, "I'm not flirting," "yes you are—enough," such was their candor and their way with each other and again His honesty only made it harder on Claudette, who only grew more fond.

(8) In the driveway she had seen Christian soften up, as it happened He had felt bad about something and apologized, seeing the soft side of this beautiful, powerful man for the first time gave her confidence to move forward. (9) Christian, feeling the moment apt, put His arm around Claudette, soon she was moving forward. (10) She started slowly on His arm and then crept closer and closer moving in the silent dark car to kiss Him. (11) Perhaps

she saw in His eyes a strength and purity that she mistook for love and being an attractive and brave girl, decided to move in for the kill. (12) She crept closer, Christian, as it started, knew where it was going, and looked on in horror wondering, "What do I do?" (13) She crept closer and not shirking away Christian finally said, "I can't tell you how bad I want to kiss and touch you," she said, "It wouldn't be anything major, doesn't have to be a big deal," but Christian knew that was a lie, He knew that attitude well and decided He wouldn't reciprocate. (14) He literally denied her, He let her continue to essentially make-out with His straight face and didn't reciprocate. (15) A little perturbed and regretful, she said goodbye to Him and He walked into the house. (16) Soon He had a missed call from her and she, after the heat of the moment, regretted what she had done, "I was feeling randy and just lost control, I'm sorry," (17) "Its ok, I get it, I wanted to do it too, I told you." (18) "It's taken Me a while to get control of myself sexually, I used to masturbate and look at porn all the time, addicted." (19) So the two bonded over the experience, Claudette trusting Christian even more now that she saw He had a lion's share of self-control. (20) Although she still wanted more in her heart, the two went on as friends.

(7) (1) One day they were riding on a bus, bonded by what they had already been through and Christian beginning to get more confident and wishing to break barriers in His relationships with women, decided to tell Claudette that she should wax her mustache. (2) He didn't know what it was, all of a sudden He's in the bus and catches sight of it, probably a few hairs, and having a familiar feeling that He sometimes got from God, like, "I know buddy, but You gotta do it," He decided to dare to be honest with her and told her. (3) "I think you should wax," brushing His hand over His upper lip. (4) Claudette, aghast, said, "Why would You say that? Oh my gosh," holding that spot on her face. (5) It wasn't that she had a mustache but that Christian knew that a guy wasn't allowed to tell a girl that that made Him decide to do it. (6) He did it for her but

just as much for Himself, to become strong and more Himself with women. (7) But as it happened, Claudette also saw His heart in it and His honesty, "Who would ever say such a thing?" (8) That quality attracted her, seeing yet again a more attractive Christian; thus their friendship continued getting more honest and comfortable. (9) Claudette found Him easier to talk to, "Since He was willing to tell me this, I know I can trust Him with anything," and the two became closer.

(10) One day Christian started to feel for some reason that the movement should be called the "Kingdom of God." (11) He wanted an all-encompassing name that would unite all Christians and for some reason He felt moved to call His movement a kingdom and even to be referred to as the King. (12) He spoke to Claudette about it, "Yeah, I'm trying to figure out should I go by a King or shouldn't I?" (13) "I think it's a bit early in the game to worry about that." (14) Christian didn't know but kept it in His heart.

(8) (1) The two grew closer, but interestingly just as friends. (2) Christian had made it clear

to her one day His stance, He was feeling a pull towards her and confessed after some text banter, “I’m afraid of falling in love with you. I’m up for falling in love with you, I just know that God told Me Sarah was the one,” (3) there’s a verse in the book of Romans that says God’s will is “good, pleasing and perfect,” (4) Christian reasoned that because God’s will was pleasing, it would be more pleasing for Him and Claudette to be friends than lovers since God had chosen Sarah for Him. (5) He encouraged Claudette to just be herself, that even if she wanted to fall in love with Him she wouldn’t because His will is pleasing. (6) So they continued a close friendship. (7) Christian also saw for the first time what a true friendship with a woman looked like; He saw in her someone that He could trust and love, no holds barred.

(8) Christian now feeling confident that He had a first member of His movement began to speak to Claudette about moving in together. (9) He was looking for a place and things having become so cool and close between them saw

a vision of them being able to work together not just as friends but now roommates.

(10) Christian would also get reveries, almost like daydreams, where His mind would take Him every which way. (11) He began to see them having application in His life, it would happen again and again, finally He reasoned it was God. (12) It was God's way of leading Him. (13) One night Christian had a reverie where He saw Himself with a woman, she was naked, but rather than it being wrong that she was naked, He felt guided by the vision to not be uncomfortable, to not be afraid of her nakedness. (14) The day came when Claudette came over, He had had this vision the night before. (15) Already sensing God's hand in these reveries and thinking them roommates soon, He knew what should happen. (16) He knew in His heart it was time for them to break the nakedness boundary. (17) They had already become close with the mustache thing but Christian knew this was next, this was a place God was calling them to go. (18) In this movement not only would cursing be as

He now saw it, but people wouldn't be weird about nakedness. (19) They wouldn't be gross about it or religious, it would just be something beautiful, normal, and He knew the place God was going to begin to set this as culture was in His friendship with Claudette.

(9) (1) Christian, ever since 14 and following God, was used to digging in His heels having to do difficult things. (2) In school that was telling people about His conversion. (3) Soon after Pittsburgh He found Himself in class next to His old friends He partied with, He would get these pangs that would tell Him, "Share with him," "Tell him about what I did for You." (4) Knowing that almost no one dared talk about God in high school if they talked at all, Christian dreaded it. (5) But knowing it was something He also wanted deep down and knowing it would make Him stronger if He did, would usually acquiesce, open His mouth, deny Himself, face His fears and speak. (6) Christian was used to this dynamic in His relationship with God knowing Jesus said, "Anyone who comes after Me must deny himself, take up his

cross daily and follow Me." (7) The same Spirit that made Him speak in 9th grade, led Him little by little to find the strength to eventually sit and speak to entire lunch tables. (8) It was as if God was stoking a flame little by little, making Him stronger and stronger. (9) The mustache thing was a similar feeling, (10) "Come on Chris, its time," He knew in His heart now as Claudette sat in His room it was now nakedness. (11) As much as you would think it fun to get naked with a hot girl, Christian still dreaded it. (12) So, knowing it was time, He looked at her from across the room. (13) Not knowing how to break the ice and begin, He noticed her thong was sticking out to her front. (14) Knowing it was God's way to give Him an in, He finally said in His heart, "Ok." He mentioned the thong, (15) "Oh my gosh, I can't believe You said that, now things are going to be weird between us," she said. (16) Christian knew however, this was perfect, "No, God doesn't want us to be weird about anything, He's been teaching Me about nakedness— its how He made us in the first place, it's not supposed to be this taboo thing. (17) We're gonna be roommates, so we've gotta get comfortable with each other in the house, can't be hiding from each other at all," "so basically we've gotta get naked." (18) "Really?" "Oh my gosh." "Listen, I'll go first." Christian, never being weird about nakedness, always actually being pretty free about it, dropped His drawers right there in front of her. (19) "You can touch it if you want," He said to her as she examined it, her also having grown up religious thus never seeing a dick in person. (20) Feeling reluctant but also like she saw a congruence of things, first with the cursing, now this, she had a real sense in her heart that this was in fact God, that He was doing and moving them to these things. (21) "Your turn," "Ugh, really?" "Fine," and though she didn't look it, she was inwardly thrilled they could do this, so half scared half thrilled she took her shirt off. (22) "You can touch it," "This is how they work yadda, yadda, if you twist it it becomes harder," she said as she twisted her nipple in her hand. (23) Christian, having only felt a girl's boob once and that time it being dark and Him being beside Himself, was grateful to now see and feel one in the light, without weirdness, where He could just be curious, be Himself. (24) Christian looked at Claudette, “Ok,” He said. “No,” she said. (25) “Claudette, trust me,” “Christian,” feeling scared but deep down knowing it was right she went to take her pants off. (26) “I’m like tribal,” she complained (about her unshaven pussy hair). (27) Christian didn’t mind though, it wasn’t about eating her out or anything sexual, He just wanted to see what a pussy looked and felt like and though He had some fears, was deep down pumped at the opportunity.

(10) (1) “Ugh, she said as she pulled her pants off, scooting back on the bed, she had her panties off but her legs closed. (2) “Claudette,” knowing she was with Him deep down and having that understanding, He gently spread her legs apart. (3) Already knowing it was cool with God, who He now knew truly was cool, looking at the heart, not being immature and stupid, began to examine her pussy. (4) Sticking His finger in it and exploring He said,

"Wow." (5) "What?" "I can't imagine how good that would feel, literally like unbelievable, I can just tell." (6) Christian was a virgin; kids at 14 weren't exactly sleeping with each other and since that's when He began following God, He just hadn't. (7) Pulling their pants up they both, though warily, moved on, both knowing it was good what they were doing, both seeing God's hand in it.

(8) Christian continued getting better and better at discerning God's voice. (9) Things were starting to develop as far as the big picture of the movement was concerned. (10) Christian continued to get impressions that He should be called a King and the movement should be called a Kingdom. (11) It was from the ether as it were, just something in the air; all of a sudden He got these strange Kingly desires. (12) Soon it would begin to make sense. (13) He was on a plane coming back from Los Angeles when He came upon a passage of scripture. (14) He was reading His Bible like He normally did, all of a sudden He got that strange uncanny feeling that He

was being spoken to by God directly. (15) He read on, "In the end times, the mountain of the house of the Lord will be raised above the other mountains, and all nations will stream to it," He read and started to understand that this movement would culminate in the actual governance of Israel, (16) that Christian would grow to became the actual temporal king of Israel! (17) The prophecy talked about a time when Israel would be sought after by all the nations, (18) Christian knew not only in His heart but also logically that this time hadn't yet arrived. (19) Number one, the world had never seen what's called the "end times," and number two, Israel had never been the leading world power in a temporal sense like the scripture was referring. (20) It was a watershed moment, Christian finally saw not only what He would become, but also the way that God truly was leading Him by His heart; He began to see that since He was anointed, He truly was being led by God through and through. (21) Christian began to identify with kings in the Old Testament. (22) When King Saul was anointed king by Samuel the prophet he was told, "Once you are anointed, do whatever your hand finds to do, for God will be with you." (23) What that meant was that once the king was anointed, God would be overseeing the inclinations of his heart and would endorse his decisions for the kingdom's sake. (24) The king would have to follow God's commands, but God would be overseeing the wisps of his heart and leading the kingdom through him as such. (25) Christian saw in a freaky way that this was happening with Him. (26) All of a sudden He just gets all these desires to be called a King, and for the movement that He would lead to be called a Kingdom, and then He gets lead to the fact that He was to be an actual King, and was to actually lead a Kingdom, (27) the internationally recognized state of Israel. (28) He saw God's hand and took comfort. (29) Mind you, even while He was getting feelings about calling His movement a Kingdom, He still believed the movement would be a church, (30) but to see how these Kingly reveries led to this prophecy and the grand narrative was truly something and it led Christian to begin to see things having to do with the nation of Israel, rather than just the church.

(11) (1) Christian was working at the time at a bagel shop. (2) He had graduated college with a degree in Industrial and Organizational Psychology, but came out with a conviction that He should do only what He truly wanted, unlike college. (3) College for Christian was almost 100 percent self-denial. (4) He went essentially because every white boy from the suburbs goes. (5) Call it pressure from family, friends, the world but it was ultimately not His choice to go to college. (6) Christian now thought college should be, if one wanted to become an engineer, he should scour the land for the best engineering school and go, but the requisite for engineering school would be a desire to become an engineer. (7) This fundamental decision Christian saw was under appreciated and in some parts lost by the grind of the world, which sometimes put the cart before the horse— choosing education, before a reason to get educated. (8) Christian saw

this as silly and backwards, and though He ground His way through college, would now would work only because He wanted to, (9) so while the rest of His friends got corporate jobs, He would work at a bagel shop. He would work a menial job that He was overqualified for until He found what He wanted.

(12) (1) His life became Claudette and Jeffery's Bagels. (2) He was fine with that because things with Claudette continued to sweeten. (3) One night they were at Christian's apartment, in His room, (4) Christian's back was hurting, so He asked Claudette to rub it for Him. (5) He sat down on His couch seat as she poured oil into her hand to rub His back. (6) He took off His shirt, and she began to work it out for Him. (7) Midway through her treatment, Christian leaned back into her, as if to be embraced. (8) Although they were friends they had become closer and closer and now with the nakedness barrier gone, He felt it was appropriate. (9) He leaned back into her and she received Him, (10) exhaling deeply she took Him in her arms and held Him. (11) She

was overwhelmed with love for this Man and this was finally a release for her. (12) She had been wanting to show her love and touch Him, and now she could. (13) She held Him for a long time, and thus began the physical relationship between them. (14) This was unique in that it was nonsexual. (15) Christian was delighted with the fact that God was showing Him a way to have a relationship with a woman, even a physical one, without romance, without a romantic prerequisite. (16) This was solely friendship and love, but the love was genuine, He truly loved this woman Claudette, and like I said, was delighted that He could get physical, even naked, with a woman without being her boyfriend. (17) They held each other, and thus began a treasured part of their relationship—cuddling. (18) That night they began something special and continued to break barriers. (19) It would be something they would go back to, something special to both. (20) They kissed as well, they didn't make-out, or use their tongues, but kissed— they would kiss maybe three or four times at a time and not infrequently. (21) It was just random, purely for love as it happened, with no direct concern to label it a certain way; both were just following God and God gave them a friendship and thus taught them what friendship could become. (22) God taught Christian that you could get naked with a friend you could even cuddle naked with a friend, even kiss and cuddle naked with a friend and it could be totally satisfying! (23) Christian was amazed that He could be naked with a woman, and still have control over Himself— to not have to be some sexual dog panting for a release. (24) He wasn't a panting dog in heat, through the toil of the way He had become sexually self-controlled over the years. He was now able to appreciate beauty, and having done it God's way and waiting, was now on top. (25) He would learn later that masturbation was ok, but God allowed Christian to be deceived in His Christian church in order to establish His discipline as a sexual man. (26) Christian started jerking off in 7th grade. (27) By 8th grade, while He was a badass, He was doing it three times a day; before He met Claudette,

He had given up masturbation completely, He hadn't jerked off in something like two years. (28) God first had to restrain the beast that was Christian's sexual appetite, to be able to teach Him it's merits, and be able to establish Christian as a sexual man, who could indeed lead and please a woman. (29) What He saw and learned was that what made women boil sexually, what make them come apart (He saw this with Claudette) was a man in control of His sexuality. (30) Christian saw that it was a man who didn't need sex, who could laugh it off, that would be the most attractive. (31) Christian saw that over the years as He sought to gain control of Himself, that not fantasizing about women He walked by on the street, started to change His attitude. (32) He saw God's hand at work, before He could learn to love a woman, He must first master Himself. (33) With His sexual appetite in check, He could now appreciate a woman, and lead her sexually-- this is how He found strength to not make-out with her in that dark car; doing it God's way, self-denial, at times brutal, fierce, self-denial was now paying dividends. (34) It was something unbelievably satisfying to be with a naked woman and a beautiful one at that, and He knew it was a reward from God after His toil and all His self-restraint over the years. (35) They began to cuddle frequently, almost every time they saw each other, perhaps 3 to 4 times a week.

(13) (1) Christian was having problems at His work and was at odds with His boss. (2) He would find out later why, but He had a terribly difficult time working, not just at this job but at almost all the jobs He ever had. (3) He just had the most difficult time dealing with people. (4) Things with the boss were rough and one day He stood up to her and was fired. (5) He wasn't a great worker, but she was also a bitch and treated Him terribly. (6) As I said, one day He stood up to her over text and told her off; being a trying worker didn't excuse the way she treated Him. (7) He was now jobless, not only jobless, but behind on His rent. (8) God was still with Him however, and this is where He found strength. (9) So He was out of work. (10) He was now free;

feeling secure spiritually, He looked ahead for the next step. (10) He was soon to be out of His house. (11) He was behind on His rent as I said, but feeling life with Him, was encouraged by Claudette. (12) Here was a girl who was fully involved in His movement who herself had money, so He began to think, "Perhaps God is leading Me to become supported by her." (13) So He kept going, and although He would soon be out of His house, He took comfort in the fact that He had someone following Him, He had a first member. (14) They had started to see each other at Claudette's house. (15) For a period however, He stayed in her car. (16) In the course of time, Christian had heard from God that Claudette should be the one to support them financially, freeing Christian up to do what He needed. (17) Christian dreaded saying this to her, but He did, and for a little while she acquiesced. (18) However, things were going south and Claudette wasn't going to support Him long term. (19) In time He found himself at the Woods-Mullen homeless shelter in Boston. (20) He was a bit scared of shelter life on the one hand, yet on the other the white boy from the suburbs in Him liked the idea of being homeless, or being without; it wasn't something He was used to— it was adventurous, something new. (21) Things got interesting quick.

(14) (1) One day He was at a soup kitchen getting lunch, all of a sudden He gets into a conversation with a Satanist. "Yeah, I know about the Illuminati, look at my book," he pulls out a leather book with a pentagram on the back, "I was brought into Satanism with my grandmother at age 5," (2) this new friend was Clarence. Christian loved him almost from the beginning. (3) "Yeah I've been to Hell multiple times." Christian had heard bullshit, but this was not bullshit, this was different, He heard it in his voice; (4) this was someone who knew what he was talking about. (5) Clarence, being familiar with Boston, showed Christian around, and they became friends. (6) One night things would take a great turn however as Christian and Clarence took to the shower. (7) All of a sudden Christian turned around to see Clarence

white eyed, (pupils turned to the back of the head) with a white sheet wrapped around his body like a robe. (8) Christian aghast, looked on wondering what was happening to His friend; (9) after a few more minutes He heard him back to himself, "What just happened?" (10) "Where did You come from? When did You get here?" (11) Christian had been watching an exorcist on Youtube some days before, and started to smell where this was going. (12) It appeared to Christian that Clarence had a demon, a real life demon that came in and out of him. (13) Christian, as He stood in the shower was giddy, seeing that God had allowed His faith to become "sight" as it were; (14) to see the real thing in person, and in shock and awe He got down under the running water and worshipped. (15) Thus began a series of demonic experiences with Clarence. (16) Clarence, who was a gentle soul, who wouldn't hurt a fly, would all of a sudden take leave of himself, would be a different person, with a different name and story. (17) He remembers one instance, "Persephone," "when were you worshipped and who worshipped you?" (18) "The Greeks." Christian after having exchanges with the spirits would look them up and find them online, He literally found "Persephone," and saw that she was indeed worshipped by the Greeks. (19) Thus was what Christian was now becoming accustomed to living alongside Clarence in this shelter. (20) It helped Him find strength in God however, He needed all the strength He could get dealing with the people there. (21) They were rough, from the street, and didn't give a fuck. (22) Christian felt powerful however; though He had left His friends and family and was perhaps thought little by them, these demons knew who He was and respected Him. (23) He would never forget when Satan himself stood next to Him. "My, my, look who it is at last. Yes, its me, before your eyes, the man himself." "So here You are, the Champion," (24) he said as he paced around Him in a circle. These experiences continued to increase Christian's faith and give Him power. (25) He remembers one night standing up to someone in the shelter. (26) "Shut up,"

Christian said, "Trying to sleep" (they all slept together in rows like in an orphanage). "What?" "What the fuck you say?" (27) "I said shut up," all of a sudden the young Spanish thug swung at Him half-heartedly, at the top bunk. (28) Such was what Christian was accustomed to in the midst of these spiritual experiences. (29) One night things became physical. (30) One of the spirits was calling himself a "dark witch" and went to physically harm Christian. (31) It moved around Christian's bed, torturing Him with scrapes and punches while the others were asleep. (32) After 20 minutes, with no one to help, and with no end in sight, Christian began to cry. (33) It was soon over and the witch was gone, but such were some of the things He went through in those days.

(15) (1) One night things got dangerous. (2) Christian was walking to the shelter from the library, all of a sudden a young black man comes up close to Him. "Buddy, I know you. Me and You are gonna fight." (3) "Why are we going to fight? What did I do?" (4) "We're gonna go to an alley and fight, and we're both

gonna go to jail." (5) Christian smelled alcohol on his breath and wasn't sure where this would go; all of a sudden the man grabs Christian by the jacket and throws Him down 10 concrete steps. (6) Christian felt the feeling of tumbling then woke up to the man, "I should kill You right now, where's my knife?" (7) "Knockout," the man said and kneed Christian in the head. "Knockout," he said, and Christian went black. (8) Next thing He knew, He was walking down the street, soon to be received at Boston Medical Center. (9) He was accosted, and it turns out the man took offense at Christian because Christian confronted him as he threw trash to the ground haphazardly some time previously. (10) It's written in the Bible about King David that certain things, after He was anointed, would fill him with rage and cause him to do extraordinary things. (11) Not just David, but multiple times in scripture, someone who was "anointed," who had the hand of God with him, would be filled with the Spirit, and be moved to do something great. (12) Clarence could see auras, could look at a person and see color radiating off them. (13) One night Christian stood up to someone in the shelter, all of a sudden was filled with rage and stared at the perpetrator in the face; Clarence later told Him, "Your aura turned to a totally different color then." (14) "Yeah, it went to a dark grey black," Christian knew that this was indeed the Holy Spirit. (15) He remembers that it was only after He was anointed that this would occur, He knew it was God inside Him that boiled in anger alongside Him. (16) Christian didn't know it at the time, but He was the leader prophesied in Revelation, who was to lead with an "iron scepter."

(16) (1) When it came to finances, Clarence was the opposite of Claudette. (2) Clarence respected Christian's authority. (3) He gladly gave Christian control, even offering to let Him hold his cards physically. (4) One night Clarence saw a vision of St. Anthony who told him to follow Christian, who said that Christian would be the way to his salvation. (5) Clarence deeply respecting spiritual things, and understanding and respecting authority, gave

it willingly to Christian. (6) Clarence Christian came to find out had extraordinary powers. (7) One day he shot an electric bolt from his hand during an argument with his mother, another time he bent an iron fence in a fit of anger. (8) One night Christian faced a certain spirit and the spirit threw an insult at Him, "You're not even human." (9) Christian was perturbed by this because though demons were obviously negative, whose words were therefore easy to dismiss, they were not often untrue. (10) "Not human?" He thought to Himself. "What do I make of that?" (11) Moved after some of the encounters, Christian being further led astray by the spirit, thought that He might be a vampire. (12) Sounds foolish, but all manner of things become reasonable when dealing with demons before your very eyes— all theories begin to deserve credence. (13) "A vampire?" Christian was bothered, and kept it in His heart. He would come to find out that He indeed was not a human, but that He was a God. (14) He learned that in the end times, there was to be five gods that would come to be on the earth. (15) God would let the world become dark, then once it reached its limit, would send these five gods into the world and then begin the "Day of the Lord" or the time of judgment against end time's sin; His judgments would lead to the setting up of a new rulership on the earth, partially the rulership of these gods, chief among them being the Christ, the one who would rule for a thousand years as Revelation says. (16) It would not be Jesus Christ who would reign for the thousand but a different man, indeed a "Christ." (17) It was Christian. He came to learn that not only was He a God, but He was a Christ. (18) Christian learned that He was indeed Soldier Christ. He was not only Christian Spalding, but before birth was alongside Jesus Christ and until 1990, when He was born, was by Jesus' side as Jesus' Son and Brother. (19) He was named "Soldier Christ" by Jesus. Christian was shown these things daily and treasured them in His heart.

(17) (1) It was winter and Christian had found a new spot to be homeless. (2) He was kicked out of the Woods-Mullen shelter for standing

up for Himself— doing what was right; He was now at the Wilson shelter in Dorchester. (3) Certain things had taken their course and He was soon staying at the Prudential shopping mall. (4) It was a nicer environment and was open 24 hours, so He made it His home. (5) He ate from the trash can during this time, not just food but drink. (6) One night at the Prudential, He found someone He recognized. (7) Months before, Christian during a stay outside in the public air, was shocked when a black man all of a sudden began kissing His face and making whimpering noises. (8) Christian thought it a mentally challenged person having compassion on Him staying outside wanting to cheer Him up, all of a sudden however, here is this same person! (9) Months later appearing. (10) Christian then knew in His heart this was an angel, not just any— His guardian. (11) It was true, this was Christian's guardian angel. (12) She came in the guise of this young black man, but it was indeed an angel, and indeed a woman named Martha, Christian would come to understand. (13) Martha began to come to

Him perhaps 3 nights in a row at the Prudential. (14) One night she came and took Him to a back room of the mall. (15) Christian was tired and Martha knowing this, sat down on the ground, motioning Christian to sit down with her; He did, then in wisdom she led Him to take His shoes and socks off. (16) She let His feet air out, also taking Him in her arms and kissing Him; she kissed His lips; shocked in a certain way, Christian who was at first tired, found Himself almost instantly rejuvenated. (17) She would pop up here and there over a few days, would say little, but was an encouraging presence; after all his demon experiences, He longed for an angel.

(18) (1) Night after night He stayed at the Prudential, waiting for God's voice, waiting for the next step. (2) In all the homelessness and the uncertainty, having God's voice was a great calm and took worry away. (3) Christian was now being shown by God that a time of peace and rest was coming. (4) This would come through His parents.

(19) (1) Christian had a mixed relationship

with His parents, sometimes liking, sometimes hating. (2) Since being homeless He generally distanced Himself from them because they thought too small and got in the way of His faith. (3) He was at odds with them a great deal of time, but now the times had changed and He thought, "Though I've been homeless all this time, about a year, maybe its time I asked them to stay." (4) Christian had liked and appreciated the distance from His family, but now it was enough, He now thought to ask them for a time of rest. (5) They agreed and soon He was on a bus to Atlanta, Georgia.

(20) (1) Living with His parents was difficult. (2) Christian went through hard times with them. He stayed with them 2 months, until there was a disagreement. (3) The disagreement left Him without a home; He decided to stand up for Himself and be homeless rather than compromise. (4) He walked 2 miles from His parents' house to Kirkwood, Georgia, along with His bags. (5) He ended up at an old church by the main street in Kirkwood, directed by God to stay there, He planted and spent the

night on the church porch. (6) He stayed there and ate people's remains in the garbage for food. (7) He stayed in Kirkwood until one day meeting His father for lunch down the street. (8) After learning that His father refused to change his mind in the disagreement, Christian got up from the meal and left. (9) He found Himself without a ride, having to make His way through Atlanta to get back to His stuff. (10) It was perhaps this day that He was directed to a parking garage when all of a sudden He felt things become different in His leadings from God. (11) He started to feel God become commanding with Him, directing Him further into the garage. (12) He understood from God now that this was His time to get "broken in," to become accustomed to Christ's authority before seeing Him in person; Christian had been told that He would indeed see God in Heaven, Christian knew this was prepping Him to be ready. (13) All of a sudden He heard God say, "Bow motherfucker," so on the concrete in the parking garage Christian got down on his knees and bowed, "Up," "Get up," "Down motherfucker," (14) the commands He was hearing got more intense and fearing God Himself, Christian, feeling this like meeting the leader of a gang, respected and followed. (15) The commands continued in His heart, "Down motherfucker," Christian feeling the intensity began not to ease Himself down, but dropping, throwing His knees and elbows into the concrete, getting up quickly and repeating the process. (16) The commands continued pounding Christian's bones and forehead into the concrete, "Down motherfucker," "Ahhhhh!" Christian cried, and began to shit and pee at the same time— terrified at the fearsome man commanding Him in His heart, but Christian feeling the commands and respecting and fearing God, continued, down and up, down and up. (17) Soon however, a guard came over to find Christian; soon an ambulance arrived, picking Him up from the ground. (18) All off a sudden Christian, strapped into the bed, heard from God, "This was him baby, wasn't Me," Christian knew this voice and knew it to be the true God of Israel, all of a sudden things made sense, that it was in fact Lucifer not Jehovah that had commanded Him. (19) "What happened to You?" The man in the ambulance asked. "I was going my way and Satan began speaking to Me, commanding me to do this and that; he commanded Me and I smashed my head into the ground obeying his commands." (20) "What's He saying Mark?" "He was spoken to by Lucifer," "Who?" (21) "Lucifer commanded Him to hurt Himself," Christian lay in the stretcher awaiting the questions, relieved to be through the torture, a feeling of relief He knew well; to be in the know— past danger. (22) "What is your name?" "Christ —, Soldier," Christian having learning recently that His name was Soldier, and that He was an ancient person, felt compelled to be truly honest with the medical workers, "Soldier, my name is Soldier," (23) "Soldier, how old are You, Soldier?" "Ancient." "What year were you born?" (24) "The year one," nervous giving this information but confident in being truly honest, He continued, now in the presence of the 21st century world. (25) The ambulance took

Him to Grady Memorial Hospital in Atlanta. "What is your name?" "Soldier." "What is your real name?" "Soldier," "Is there any ID on Him?" "No," "He says His name is Soldier." (26) "Soldier, do You know what happened to You?" (27) "I was attacked by Lucifer who was commanding Me, I know it sounds crazy but you know those people who say the Devil told them to do this or that— like that." (28) "He told Me to get up and get down viciously, and I obeyed, thinking it was God," (29) "Ok." They took Christian to the 13th floor of Grady, the psychiatric wing. (30) Soon He was taken into the more intense section of the 13th floor, where He was given a bed and forced to stay.

(21) (1) He would hold that His name was Soldier for a long time, until God would signal otherwise, which He did, counseling Him to go with Christian as His name until the time was right. (2) Christian acquiesced, and was counseled further that God wanted Him to lay claim to the incident as a psychiatric episode, that He had indeed heard a voice like a delusion. (3) He understood by God that

though He was this Messiah, that God wanted Him to admit Himself as someone who had been mentally ill for His purposes. (4) Feeling unable to go anywhere else and trusting God, He admitted Himself and began to say it was a "delusion" that He had been under. (5) He felt led by God to say that this delusion, which had become violent only recently, was what He began to follow at 14! (6) He gave them a story, lying to them, in order to accomplish something greater. (7) Ultimately because they would not accept that Christian was just following God; they would not let Him out of the mental wing without giving Him a diagnosis, claiming that it was for His "good and well-being." (8) Christian knew it was because this world had unseen authorities, authorities that had real control. (9) He knew it was because this world was enslaved by the Devil that He was locked up in this wing. (10) Why did He need to be held against His will by this hospital? (11) He was fine, and was ready to go home, but finding Himself in the mental wing, simply would not be released; He learned that He simply did not have the ability to leave, He literally could not leave the hospital if He wanted to. (12) Knowing this ultimately was Satan's work on the 21st century world, a place where people were not trusted ultimately, He acquiesced to God's ultimate hand in leading Him and submitted to the doctors— allowing Himself to be thought mentally ill.

(22) (1) He followed the doctors and went to classes, and did stupid things; things that a retard would do, He did, knowing who's hand led Him. (2) He would stay in the mental wing for about a week. (3) One night He was forced to take Triscanal, a drug. (4) He woke up later that night feeling like He'd had a lobotomy. (5) He looked into the mirror at His droopy eyes as He felt His brain disconnected from the rest of His consciousness. (6) In His heart He groaned, looking to God for relief, "When will You lead me out?" (7) But knowing and feeling the presence of God with Him, He kept going, allowing Himself to be thought ill, owning this past "mental illness" for God. (8) Again the story being that He had become

delusional when He was 14, when He was in Pittsburgh; He began this delusion then and didn't know it was a delusion until He fucked Himself against the concrete. (9) And that after the violent incident now saw that it had all been a delusion that He followed and was thus no longer delusional; that was the story He was led to give the doctors. 10) And thus because His clearing from the delusion was mental, He didn't need physiological relief through medication.

(23) (1) Soon His parents were called and He was released from the hospital with a "diagnosis," and a tube of pills. (2) Christian now having a better rapport with His parents, told them about the Triscanal, how terrible it was, and without telling them dumped out the pills as soon as He had the chance at the house. (3) That night after being locked up against His will for two weeks, He decided to get some fresh air. (4) As He was walking back home, after walking about two miles, He experienced something He'd never experienced before; the landscape literally changed around Him.

(5) He was walking in the night, everything was normal, feeling it time to turn around and go back home He turned around and literally found Himself looking at a road that He didn't recognize! (6) Christian having learned of angels and things supernatural through His demon experiences was excited as He dealt with this new reality; that He was now separated from His parents by God with nothing He could do. (7) With no way to get back to His house, He walked on. (8) He walked, stopping briefly to masturbate in the grass— moving forward. (9) He stripped down naked in the grass near where the landscape changed and jerked off in the night air. (10) It was partially the fact that the landscape changed that He felt so free, so free from the concerns of this world and so close to God that He could do such a thing. (11) He walked on, back through Atlanta, following God now free from the difficult and spiritually incompetent 21st century medical world He had been entrenched in.

(24) (1) He wandered. (2) God had taught Him that He was special and referred to

Him frequently as Peter Pan. (3) Peter Pan could fly and was magical. One time during the wandering, Christian started to hear God start leading Him to a scary place. He was in a lesson with God, learning about how sin should be atoned for and it was time for Him to pay for His. (4) God would now call Him to account for His sin or so He thought. (5) It was a mysterious moment for Him, because although He didn't know the ins and outs in the moment, His gut told Him something, and there comes a time when your gut tells you and you just know, these moments Christian knew well, and if there was ever a person to listen to them, it was Christian. (6) Christian was walking but all of a sudden He felt the draw in His heart that He had to punish Himself for some of His past sin, it was treating black people and others under His class system as less important, racism essentially. (7) Because of perhaps something He did long ago, it was now time for Him to pay. (8) He all of a sudden had a clear message that He needed to get on to the ground and needed to bash out one of His teeth. (9) He gets down on the sidewalk and begins to question it in His heart. When He looked to God, God told Him, "Chris, this is the road to becoming Peter." (10) Feeling that uncanny feeling that it had to be done, He did, He went to knock one of His teeth out. (11) He wriggled and writhed for about 15 minutes, scraping the sides of His head by His eyebrows and He did it; all of a sudden, an ambulance showed up. (12) "He's got blood all over," they handcuffed Him, not knowing if He might hurt Himself again and they led Him to Atlanta Medical Center. (13) Christian spent the night under the lamp, getting stitched up on both sides of His head, but would never forget what He noticed when He looked in the mirror the next day. (14) He noticed a certain sheen and texture to His gaze, a certain fineness that hadn't been there before, a spiritual purity that He knew could only now show forth. (15) Christian understood that in the universe, spirituality doesn't play games; if you want to be the real deal, you will have to pay, He knew that what He went through was a purification;

(16) in that moment and soon after God made it clear to Him it wasn't prejudice that made God walk Him into that psychological area, but it was to purify Him. (17) Christian had to face His fears. Even by facing them and thinking thoughts for a millisecond, they were admissible in the spiritual ether. (18) It was the fear of pain that He purged in the incident. At one point He thought in that moment, "I should drag My nails against the pavement so as to rip one of them off." Then facing His fear by then dragging them. Although He might have had one or two questions, seeing the purity in His gaze now in the mirror He had none.

(25) (1) He was soon back at home and now things were different with the parents. (2) They now had a parameter in order for Him to stay, He would need to attend a class. (3) It was called "Moving Forward," a class for those who were recently in the mental health system— a transitional class, moving them into the "real world." Christian in order to keep His spot with them, decided He would go.

(26) (1) Every Monday, Wednesday, and

Friday, Christian would attend this horrible class where they basically drew pictures and talked about them. Trudging along through the mental health world for God, Christian kept going, knowing He had done nothing wrong.

(27) (1) One day His mom and dad came to pick Him up from class. Christian had decided to take a walk and was a block or so from where He was usually picked up. Catching His father off guard, Christian saw His expression for Him, one of contempt. (2) It was like seeing how a person would treat you if they didn't know you were looking at them; Christian saw His father treat Him with a disgusting contempt just by His face. (3) Christian rode back to the house in silence as He considered half-warily what this might mean. (4) Coming home, He felt in His heart it was time to stand up to His father. (5) He felt that His father was bullying Him by the contempt that he had in his heart and knowing how God was putting person by person under Him, He knew it was His dad's turn. (6) Christian went to His email and wrote it out, "You wanna take the gloves off, lets take

the fucking gloves off," He continued, "I dare you to lay a hand on Me, please I beg of you, I'm the Son of God, you have no idea who you're talking to." (7) He wrote two emails sticking up for Himself, challenging him. (8) After writing both emails He went off, walking down the street to Barnes and Noble. In the comics section where He'd recently become accustomed, all of a sudden a black woman in her thirties with a utility belt, gun, and a uniform addressed Him, "Christian Spalding? Come with us." (9) Putting the book down, He slowly walked to the front of the store and out the door. (10) "We came to make sure everything was alright, we heard from your father that things weren't going so hot," "We're gonna take you to Grady Memorial hospital, just to get a reading on you, make sure you're doing alright." (11) Christian now realized His dad had called the authorities after being perturbed by the emails. (12) Rubbing His head exasperated, Christian spoke to the paramedic, "If I have to, I guess I'll go, but I'd rather go home." Resigned, "Whatever I have to do," and they were off. (13) Pulling into the emergency room, Christian was led out of His straps and seat. (14) He came to a room with many people, a crowded ER. And with no supervision any longer by those who brought Him, He thought of a plan. He thought, "These people brought Me here for no reason, now they want Me to wait in a crowded waiting room to see a doctor." (15) (In the waiting room He was given a bracelet and told to wait, He sensed He would have to wait an hour or so) Feeling the go ahead from God, He decided to do it, He was going to walk out. (16) He was going to bite the plastic bracelet off His wrist and walk out. Twiddling His thumbs, about to make the final call, He did it, deciding to walk out, even in the midst of all the hubbub earlier. (17) Soon He was walking down the street towards Georgia State University, giddy in His heart for accomplishing this brave thing. (18) God spoke to Christian then and made known to Him that this was indeed like David, this is something David would have done, walking out, sticking up for himself. (19) He walked down the street, not knowing exactly what the next step would be. He knew He couldn't go back to His parents.' All of a sudden He had a plan; He would call His old best-friend Rich, making an appeal for him to drive from Nashville to come get Him. (20) He needed a phone however, and finding someone, He said, (21) "Let me borrow your phone, I have to make one call, in a tight spot," catching a compassionate stranger, He was given the phone. (22) Dialing His friend He found him on the line, "Christian! What's up?" (23) "Listen, I need you to get in your car and literally drive to Atlanta and pick me up, my dad just went King Saul on me—threatening me, I need you to come and get me," "Where are you?" "GSU on Gilmer Street," (24) "Alright." "I'll be waiting here in the student union for you to come, meet Me like I said on Gilmer," "Alright." (25) Giving the phone back, Christian got up, heading into the student center. (26) Feeling He was in the clear somewhat, He sat down to watch TV, waiting for His friend to arrive. All of a sudden He finds His dad there on His left appearing out of nowhere! (27) “Christian,” he sat down, “What is going on? I am your best friend, no one else supports You like I do, what is the problem?” (28) Instead of coming straight, Rich called Thomas, and Thomas called his dad, telling him where Christian was. (29) “I told you I am now Father to you, and what we went through we needed to go through,” Christian told him. Christian had written His family months before, telling them how He had been called by God and how He was given authority, and telling them He was now to be Father to all of them. (30) “Remember what I told you? God has made me a Father to you, and we needed to go through these things to set that in place.” (31) Understanding in his heart what Christian said, he coaxed Him, and Christian agreed to spend the night back at the house. (32) Christian had learned what it meant to have someone under Him in Boston with Claudette, but even more so with Clarence. (33) Christian was amazed at how God didn’t play, that when God gives power He really means it, that power is power; He remembers feeling absolute power over Clarence, that He was literally His slave. He was amazed that God had given a person into His control. (34) Christian now knew that God was putting His own father under Him. (35) After the whole incident Christian went to bed, pleased that God had now put His father under His foot. (36) Adam went to bed pleased as well, knowing that God's hand was with his Son, knowing that through the chaos of the day, it all made sense; (37) what was in his heart towards his Son had to be exposed, and Christian had to stand up to him to put everything in place. (38) He was up late the next morning; all of a sudden there was a knock at the door. "Hello?" "Can I come in?" "Christian?" (39) "I was called by Grady hospital last night, why didn't You show up?" (40) "They came to Me in the middle of Barnes and Noble and asked to rush Me to the ER, even though I had done nothing, after seeing how crowded it was, and seeing I had to wait I said, 'Fuck this, I've done nothing, am I just gonna wait here for them? No,' so I left." (41) Well, we're gonna need to take You back for testing to make sure everything is ok." Christian then found out they had called a 1043 on Him, which is a code that gives the police the authority to seize a person if they have had a mental health diagnosis and take them to a hospital, even against their will for an allotted time in order to get them medicated or treated somehow. (42) Knowing there was nothing He could do about it, He acquiesced, and was soon in another stretcher in another ambulance headed to Grady hospital. (43) He got there to find the same room now with less people, and soon He saw the doctor. (44) "We're gonna take some blood from You and have You see a doctor just to make sure everything is ok," (45) "But why? What have I done? My father and I had a disagreement, we got over it last night, you are doing this for no reason." (46) "Sir, we just need to make sure everything is alright." Christian knew in His gut He couldn't win, He knew the system was too fucked up, that simply because He had been in the hospital before, the police had probable cause giving them authority to lock Him up. (47)

Knowing the real reason and knowing God's ultimate hand in allowing all of this, He acquiesced and went along, drudging the fact that God was leading Him once again into the mental health world. (48) They stripped Him down, gave Him a robe, and soon He was back on the 13th floor to face His sentence. (49) Like His first visit, He knew He now had to face doctors and go through the whole rigamarole once again. This time however, feeling He had support from His father, He sought to be rescued over and over. (50) On the 13th floor they had Him wait for three days. In a robe with nothing other than socks, He waited, angry that He was being locked away having done nothing. (51) He knew that this was all just 21st century bullshit, one person reacting fearfully to the next and doing stupid things out of protocol. (52) Christian was amazed that a college graduate, who was extremely normal, even above average in many ways, was stripped of so many of His rights, and given such a low seat in society. (53) He was now again at the mercy of the system; He was a mental case, and in anger He looked at God trying to discern the reason. (54) Three days later He was moved to Georgia Regional Hospital, a larger mental hospital where they move people from the 13th floor, a residential hospital, where a person is kept until they are medicated and found housing. (55) He would never forget the ride to Georgia Regional. (56) They put Him in a sort of straight jacket and put cuffs on His feet. (57) He had to walk three straight minutes as the cuffs dug into His heels. (58) He complained, "They're on too tight," but they did nothing for Him, and He walked on in pulsing pain. (59) Soon He was in a recliner chair watching TV. This section lasted two days. (60) He was soon in the regular residence of the hospital with His unit. (61) He was unit 15, sharing a section of the hospital with 18 other patients. It was a time of training and spiritual development. (62) God would use the TV and the sounds near His room to teach Him, preparing Him for what was ahead. (63) One time things got weird with the staff, He seemed to feel spiritual murkiness in the air and He sensed something was not right. (64) It was as if God opened the lid of Hell, letting demons come to play through the staff, so it was like they weren't themselves when they interacted with Him. (65) One time a whole group of them grabbed ahold of Him and shoved Him this way and that, finally pinning Him to the ground by His bed, giving Him two shots in the ass. (66) It was confusing, Christian had no idea why they were doing this, what the real reason was; but such were the things He became accustomed to at first.

(28) (1) One day He was in the cafeteria and noticed a girl from across the way. She wasn't a 10 per-say, but she was cute and attractive, and He couldn't take His eyes off her. (2) The next day or so He was in an activity with the rest of them (the patients engaged in classes during the day) and He heard the girl speak. Turns out the girl was the sister of someone Christian knew as a child, she was actually the older sister of a girl He had had a crush on as a ten year old! (3) He told her, "You're Sandra, Sandra Mitchells." "Yes," "I knew your sister

at camp as a kid, I had a huge crush on her," "Huh," thus was the start of a friendship and romance between them. (4) Soon Christian told her that it wasn't her sister that He wanted, but her, and she felt the same. (5) They both felt that God had His hand in linking them together. (6) Having Sarah there made time pass and gave His heart something to settle on. He would long to see her, waiting sometimes all day for His unit to get to see hers; but they did it, they had a hospital romance. (7) They would sneak kisses and hold hands when they could. (8) Christian saw that God was there for Him through her especially. (9) It would turn out that this girl was the girl from Revelation 12. (10) In that passage, there's a prophesied woman who would be with child, who would have a child who would come to rule the world; the "having a child" part is figurative, it just means helping "give birth" to a person, this man, by believing in Him when no one else would. (11) This woman was Sandra and the child was Christian. (12) Christian was told by God earlier that He would have multiple wives, so He told Sarah; they spoke very frankly about all things and no differently about the future. (13) She was a brief joy in Christian's life, but just like that she was gone, she left the hospital— discharged.

(29) (1) The days dragged on and Christian felt boredom more than anything. (2) Sometimes His family came to visit Him which most of the time He dreaded. (3) During one of the meetings with His dad present, He was asked about what brought the hospitalization about, and He told the story in front of His dad, "I felt I was being bullied by my dad and the only thing I could do to defend myself was to stand up to him," (4) "It was like two alpha males struggling under one roof, these things just have to play out sometimes," (5) they all seemed to understand, and Christian was grateful for an opportunity to make things right even further with His dad. (6) But He still had to face the days alone, He had to make the most of things, in fact He was gaining weight. (7) He put on like fifteen pounds because food was His only source of goodness at the time.

(8) He cherished mealtime because it was a chance to leave everything behind and enjoy something, so he ate and ate. (9) He still felt so abused and so mistreated in that hospital, sitting there being treated by many as a patient, as an idiot sometimes, when He had done literally nothing. (10) He was innocent, yet God decided to put Him in chains in the psychiatric system. (11) He was incredibly bored most of the time, so one day He decided He would read; He had a Bible there, and thought He would read it like never before— from cover to cover. (12) He had read the Bible daily for years but never read it like a narrative starting from the beginning, so this is what He did. (13) Over the course of a week or two He started in Genesis and ended in 2 Kings— cruising. (13) Sandra, who was released, would call the hospital to speak with Him, it was usually a thrill to get a call from her, though sometimes He dreaded it. (14) Sandra was still coming out of the world, still waking up to the realities of the spiritual world— that God is real, that Satan is the enemy— the basics of being a

Christian. (15) These were things Christian was well versed in but Sarah new to. (16) Christian had inspired her in this new path to see these things clearly. (17) Sometimes He would dread phone calls with here, where she would just talk on and on lifelessly. (18) But He hung with her, knowing God had a plan in it, knowing her antics would someday clear but most of all knowing they had a future. (19) Christian was once again forced to take drugs. (20) It was now something other than Triscanal, and God had counseled Christian to fake taking them. (21) They were administered in the morning and at night and Christian would take it, pop it into His mouth, and quickly move it between His top lip and teeth, storing it there until He could throw it away. (22) He got good at this and in the end took very few pills.

(30) (1) The 21st century psychiatric state of things was nothing short of slavery. (2) They would take in people, many of them kids from a lower class, who had acted out in some way, say they had a disorder then give them medication which was sometimes a chemical lobotomy.

(3) Christian was there with patients who had ailments but which were of a spiritual nature, not physiological. (4) He was with people who needed to become Christians and give their lives to God, not who needed medication. (5) Christian got a true dose of the mental hospital— well accustomed to outcries from patients who acted out this way and that. (6) But He kept to Himself— seeing and knowing God was with Him. (7) Christian knew that this was all part of His training— He knew in His heart He would be great, and this was the pathway; (8) the world needed a leader who would truly understand systems like the psychiatric and understood the ailments of society, who could relate to these underrepresented people. (9) Funny thing, on the walls of the hospital were posters expressing a patient's right to refuse medication, but if one did, they would call security who would use shots to sedate them. (10) They did not play when it came to drugs, if the "doctor ordered it" you took it and you couldn't refuse. It was ugly, but God through Christian's sneaking allowed a through-way.

(31) (1) One night Christian woke up to the sound of a black guy making a fuss outside His door. He was being loud and complaining; he had a deep voice and Christian knew it was going to wake up the whole wing if he didn't quiet down. (2) Christian listened to him say that he was from Chicago, from the Gangster Disciples and similar things that terrified Him. (3) Christian was afraid of black people. He wasn't afraid of them, every one of them, He loved them, but He knew that they were the oppressed people of His time, and that this oppression led some to become violent. (4) Christian noticed it almost daily in His dealings with them, He couldn't so much as make eye contact with some of them on the street, without causing them to become aggressive. (5) Black people who were evil would look at white oppression and would thus hold every white person accountable by bullying him. (6) In many ways in Christian's world, black people were the champions and if you didn't bend to their strength they might hurt you. (7) This was the world Christian was used to, and as

a white person, He was either to fall victim or fight back, and fighting back meant risking His life sometimes. (8) This is why He hated black people. (9) On this night that He heard this man crying out, He had a feeling He knew well. God would sometimes put Christian in situations where He was the only one who could make things right and would keep up trouble until He acted. (10) Christian waited in His bed trying to discern if this was one of these. It turned out it was. Christian knew that He could stop the man's moaning but it would cost Him, He would have to stand up to Him ever so slightly, complaining that He was keeping Him awake. (11) Finally, begrudgingly, He got out of His bed, came to the open room and told the man, "Bro you're keeping me awake, you're too loud, trying to sleep," "Oh my bad man," the man took it totally differently than Christian feared; he was apologetic, and nothing came to blows like Christian feared. (12) These two would become friends, Christian heard from God that this would be a special man and would have a mighty impact on his black world.

(32) (1) The days continued to pass and soon Christian was out, the day had finally come, He had been in this Hell for almost two months. (2) They were the longest two months of His life. (3) But He was out and back with His parents. (4) As I said, Christian had learned from God that He was a Christ, that He was the Son and Brother of God, thus, this put Him in a predicament with His parents. (5) How would He refer to them? His mother had birthed and raised Him, but principally, He had no mother, like the angels He was born of God, given life by a Father solely. (6) The time came when Christian began to call His parents by their first names. (7) It was difficult at first and they fought it a bit, but in the end He began to call them “Adam” and “Tricia.”

(33) (1) He was home not long, a few weeks, and then received a call from a group home for the aged or disabled. (2) Bricks-Watson House would be his new home. As miserable as it was being among the “mentally disabled,” Christian was grateful to be on His own, away from His parents. (3) They were still coming out

of the spiritual cob webs of their proud white world and would get Christian tangled in it; He wanted space from them. (4) He also became a beneficiary of Social Security Disability and began for the first time in almost three years to receive an income. (5) He spent His days at this new place, bored mainly— sitting in His room doing nothing. (6) Soon however, a new passion began growing in Him, He started to get into technology. (7) Christian was told by God that part of His path to becoming King over Israel was first becoming a CEO; He knew that He would one day be lord of a conglomerate. (8) He somehow knew in His heart however, that the conglomerate would start in technology, that He would be a certain fusion of Steve Jobs and Steve Wozniak. (9) He had a desire to get to know computers and technology down to the atom. He dreamed of becoming a hacker— one who knew the ins and the outs of computers from the hardware to the software. (10) God began to teach Him electronics, starting from electricity itself. (11) Christian wanted to have a full-fledged understanding of all things electric, He wanted to be the Father of electricity. (12) At one time in the past, God had actually made it known to Him that "Tony Stark" or "Iron Man" was a commercialization of the Messiah whom He was. (13) It was soon four months at the Bricks-Watson house, and Christian was starting to get a view of the next chapter. (14) Christian thought He was destined to stay in Atlanta and begin things with Sandra. He knew that she in fact was the Revelation 12 woman, and living in Atlanta where she was, figured it would be the next step. (15) That the "birthing" would be her believing in Him, He thought that she would play a role in being the first to call Him Soldier— His heavenly name, the one given by God. (16) But God had made it known to Christian that He would indeed send Him back to Boston, to give Him a city to blossom in, and to rejoin Him with Claudette and Clarence. (17) He was told that Clarence would become His servant. (18) He rejoiced at the thought. (19) In His wisdom, God had already set in motion a master, servant relationship with Clarence in Boston, so it would work swimmingly to resume it. (20) It would be a joy to live with Him and Christian thought it an honor to, like the prophets of the Old Testament, have a servant. (21) He was also told that it would be Claudette who would be his first wife. (22) Claudette and Christian had since stopped talking. (23) In Boston they stopped communicating. It was around the time Christian began going to the Woods-Mullen shelter. (24) Claudette was a bit paranoid and one day she began to get scared and fearful of Christian, (25) she acting on the side of shakiness and fear, decided to call the cops and get a restraining order. (26) The fact is, she was running from God and acting frantic, there was no real reason, Christian hadn't earned it. (27) Christian was very crafty and wise in His dealings and she would get overwhelmed by the breadth of His intellect and somehow, one day just had enough and went to the police, trying to find some way to control Him. (28) Although in Boston Christian thought about her much, since the restraining order, He barely thought of her, but was now told God would bring her back. (29) The way that He would get to Boston would be the lottery. Christian knew that He would indeed become prime-minister of the state of Israel and then convert the nation's government into a monarchy, like that of Qatar, but He would indeed become great before that, becoming rich. (30) The way He was told was the lottery; instead of needing to make His money by a product or a company, God would give Him start-up capitol by the lottery. (31) Christian knew He would be rich ever since God told Him when He was homeless. (32) He remembers walking the streets of Boston penniless, when God told Him that He would be rich; it was like a storybook, the poor street rat growing into a king and rich man, like Jean Valjean. (33) It was an exciting prospect and it was now coming to fruition in Atlanta through the lottery.

(34) This is the story of the Christ.

Psalms of Christian as He wrestled with life and with God between 2014 and 2015

(34) November 22, 2014

(1) Comfort Me My God. (2) I am under pressure on every side. (3) I desire a woman, To kiss and touch her boobs. (4) I want the rush from the firmness and softness of her boobs to comfort Me. (5) Waking up that seems the most appealing thing. (6) I miss Sarah. (7) I go on her profile and look through her pictures missing her. (8) God be My comfort.

(35) December 9, 2014

(1) I am weary of God. (2) I'm afraid to read My Bible, afraid to keep going. (3) Pain is what I see in front of Me. Deep throbbing pain feels ahead of Me and my soul is weary of it. (4) God I'm scared. (5) When will I reach green grass? When will I see sunlight? (6) When will My decisions be deeply validated? (7) I am weary of You God.

(36) January 22, 2015

(1) My heart is calloused. (2) My thirst is gone.
(3) My Bible is a burden. (4) My days wane on.

(37) January 23, 2015

(1) There is none like You. (2) In silence You silence Me. (3) You have blessed Me My holy God. (4) There is none like You.

(38) February 5, 2015

(1) I have no faith. (2) I am under unbelievable pressure. (3) I can't even think. (4) I have been robbed of all My freedom. (5) The enemy rapes Me, humping Me like a horny dog. (6) Again, again, again. (7) There is no silence.

(39) March 21, 2015

(1) I'd like to kill Myself. (2) My days feel like they are slipping away from Me. Like I'm unable to catch a full breath. (3) I just want peace, just want green, just want clearing. (4) God help Me. (5) Break through fog, strengthen Me.

(40) March 31, 2015

(1) I feel terrible. (2) I feel finding and learning from God in the morning like lifting a 200lb bar. (3) I want to just shoot Myself. (4) I feel like deadweight taking up space.

(41) June 23, 2015

(1) I am gross. (2) I feel like shit. (3) I miss Claudette incredibly.

(42) July 7, 2015

(1) I feel like a piece of shit. A living piece of shit literally. (2) I have one contact lens, bad haircut, no money. (3) My job is to embarrass Myself each day. (4) Show me the next way I need to embarrass Myself God. Show Me the next way I need to suffer. (5) My job is to be the piece of shit for the world.

(43) September 28, 2015

(1) I hate My life. I don't want to be cheered up. (2) What am I doing? (3) I am alone. (4) Where is help? What am I doing? (5) Where are you God? Where are you God.

(44) October 30, 2015

(1) I literally do not want to live. (2) I wouldn't put up a fight if caught by a mob. (3) My life is walking a tight rope of wire hair thin. I cannot breathe here. (4) Everything around is deception and trap. (5) Who is not against Me? Literally everyone I know is against Me. (6) The entire underworld against Me. (7) I have nothing; I'm poor, wretched, ripped jeans, cold, in a shit whirlwind. (8) Fledgling, beaten, bruised, limping, barely making it; where God, where are You? You hide and make Me suffer. (9) I have no clearing; the world despises Me, the invisible world as well and You watch silently, folding Your hands watching, You watch, comfortable in Your house as I slip in shit and lie cold, wind drying shit to skin, cold. (10) You watch Me and do nothing. (11) Come before I'm eaten alive, before dogs eat Me alive who wait on My life. (12) Dogs are around me, ravenous dogs, snarling eager to rip Me apart;

(13) ONE WRONG STEP, RIP HIS FUCKING SKIN APART, rip this Fucker in half. (14) All around snarling, I walk, tiptoeing, barely clothed, cold, tiptoeing in between glass, cold, wind beaten, hungry, lonely, alone in darkness; shaking, barely making it, looking for You as You silence Yourself, barely breathing as You watch in silence, holding back comforters, (15) “NO Stop! Don’t! Don’t comfort, NO!” (16) You watch Me and do nothing.

(45) November 2, 2015

(1) I want to die. (2) I don't want to be here. (3) Don't want to live anymore. (4) Bored, tired, unhappy, struggling most of the time. (5) I am impatient with God, I want Him to hurry up and get Me the fuck out of this shit hole. (6) I'm discouraged, a low Vagabond enjoying little, just wafting here and there.

(46) January 16, 2015

(1) How long, Lord? (2) How long will I live and every day have sorrow in My heart? How much shall I sigh? (3) Come quickly, God, Lord, Father, help. Please come. (4) Come my Lord and God; come, My Lord, Father God.

(47) November 15, 2015

(1) Jehovah, My God, do not be far from Me. Be very close, do not let Me out of your sight. (2) I am endangered, vulnerable, a sheep, white, clear-eyed, plump, walking amidst wolves. (3) I am scared, afraid to go freely. (4) I am terrified, horrified, at My ruthless enemy; vulnerable and weak; I am in need, defenseless, vulnerable, (5) an easy target.

(6) Be close Jehovah, wipe this fucker off the face of the earth; take him by the collar and bash him ruthlessly into the wall, draw blood, beat him shitless, make him retreat in fear, (7) bash him, drive him far from Me. (8) I hate him, I hate violence, wipe it far from Me and My eyesight. (9) Come quick, do this, spare Me, I am vulnerable and in need. Save Me, quick, please, come rescue Me from my powerful enemy, from this one more powerful than Me. (10) Come quickly, glorify yourself, rescue Me. (11) Come quick My Lord and my God.

(48) December 5, 2015

(1) I hate My miserable life. (2) I would rather be dead and not alive, not here. (3) Its too difficult, too hard, to struggle at all times with no relief. (4) Struggling all the time, that is My life. Why should I keep going? What good is it? (5) Somebody come end it for me please so I can breath. I hate My life and do not want to breath anymore. (6) Rescue me My God. Before I die, before I lose, help please, My Lord God, My Father, and Friend.

(49) January 26, 2016

(1) I hate You. (2) This is excruciating. (3) I'm worn out, spent, tired, and miserable. (4) I hate Myself and My life, hate it completely. (5) I hate You and all You plan for Me to suffer through, I hate it with a powerful hatred. (6) Care little for anything in the future. What do I have but vague wisps of destiny; mirages, that cannot help Me. (7) Misery is My faithful friend.

Printed in the United States
by Baker & Taylor Publisher Services